For my sister Christa

In the light of the moon
a little egg lay on a leaf.

One Sunday morning the warm sun came up and – pop! – out of the egg came a tiny and very hungry caterpillar.

He started to look for some food.

On Tuesday
he ate through
two pears,
but he was
still hungry.

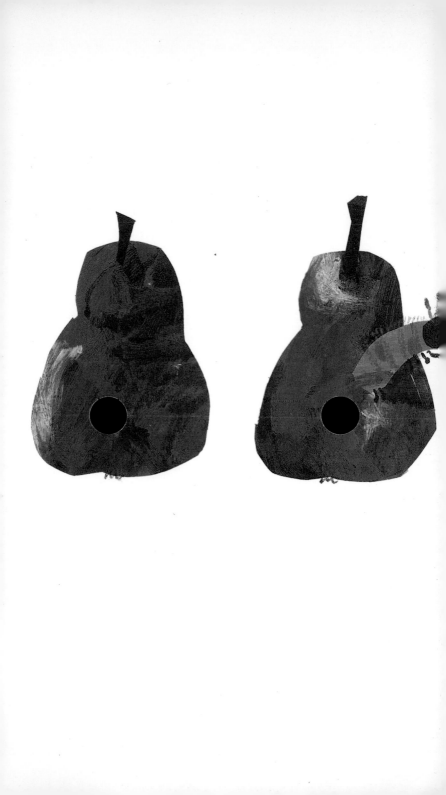

On Wednesday
he ate through
three plums,
but he was still
hungry.

On Thursday
he ate through
four strawberries,
but he was still
hungry.

On Friday
he ate through
five oranges,
but he was still
hungry.

On Saturday
he ate through
one piece of
chocolate cake, one ice-cream cone, one pickle, one slice of Swiss cheese, one slice of salami,

one lollipop, one piece of cherry pie, one sausage, one cupcake, and one slice of watermelon.

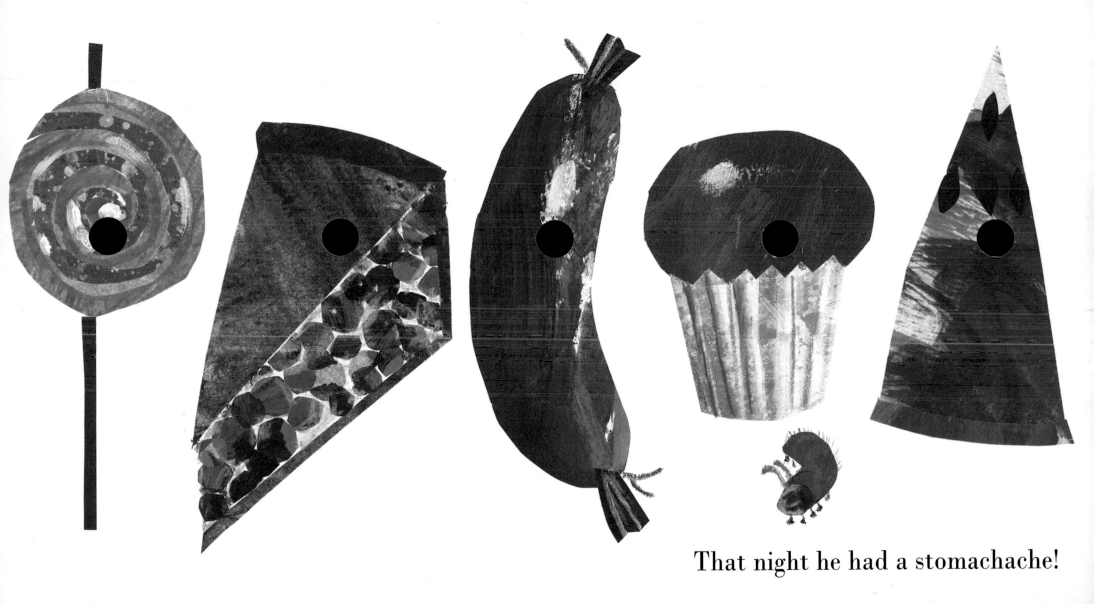

That night he had a stomachache!

The next day was Sunday again.
The caterpillar ate through
one nice green leaf,
and after that he felt
much better.

Now he wasn't hungry any more – and he wasn't a little caterpillar any more.
He was a big, fat caterpillar.

He built a small house, called a cocoon, around himself. He stayed inside for more than two weeks. Then he nibbled a hole in the cocoon, pushed his way out and ...

he was a beautiful butterfly!

Some other picture books by Eric Carle

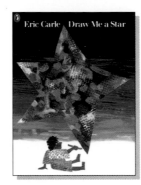

PUFFIN BOOKS

Published by the Penguin Group: London, New York, Australia, Canada, India, Ireland, New Zealand and South Africa
Penguin Books Ltd, Registered Offices: 80 Strand, London WC2R 0RL, England

puffinbooks.com

First published in the USA by The World Publishing Company, Cleveland and New York, 1969
Published in Great Britain by Hamish Hamilton Ltd 1970
Published in Picture Puffins 1974
Published in this edition 2002
042

Manufactured in China by South China Printing Co, Ltd

ISBN – 13: 978–0–140–56932–2

To find out more about Eric Carle, visit his web site at www.eric-carle.com